I0831311

Pent-O-Gramme

(1) The Worlds LONGEST Day (S.A.S)

(2) The BUTTER Melted in Anneka's Mouth

(3) Carted off to the Carlton

(4) Paulie Dee's Magazine with Oprah & the Queen

(5) MAYHEM

All available at www.LuLu.com

MAYHEM can be seen Everywhere, from Supermarket Ques to the Dog Getting off the lead but in Psychiatric Hospitals and Jails bringing this to a Pinnacle. Paul was a Bright Young Intelligent Male who from an Early Age Realized he had the same Initial's as The Police Northern

The B.I.G.A. CLEARER Perfect Picture.

The Worlds LONGEST Day

The Day I Took One and Ten

S.A.S

Imagination

Knowledge = SUCCESS

What is your B.I.G.A. picture

What is your CLEARER picture

& what is your Perfect Picture

Way Back then...the early days.

Paulie and R.O.Y.G.B.I.V. (The first known Octowarrior) were born in a place called Carlisle. Carlisle is also known as the Great Border City which lies in the North West of England within the County of Cumbria. Cumbria has some stunning views especially around the Lakes (Windermere, Grassmere & Keswick) being some of their towns. There is a wide variety of people who reside here in Cumbria where we try to achieve tranquillity.

Although Carlisle is known as an English City there has been times throughout History when it was occupied by the Scottish. Within the Roman Empire Hadrian built a wall from West to East giving a Scottish, English boundary. The wall still stands in part with fell walkers and other tourists walking this countryside seeing for themselves the Roman Remains. This wall is commonly known as Hadrian's Wall or the Roman Wall.

Both Paulie & R.O.Y.G.B.I.V. could be mischievous in their younger days and sometimes found themselves in trouble with the LAW (Never an Angel). They thought they could do as they pleased and the Police occasionally had to point them in the right direction.

Paulie did of course have a lot of good to offer and the more he thought of this the more his life progressed.

Whilst moving to a small town on the outskirts of the the City called Longtown, Paulie was still naive as to what lay on his path.

MAYHEM

Being the oldest Son of a Freemason with his Mother from the farming community, Paulie has witnessed much in life.

His Father Kenneth and his Mother Celia never married and Kenneth tried to deny responsibility of Paulie but his Mother stands by her words forty years on.

Kenneth's Father owned some land which he held caravans on and Celia's parents had a small holding called Rangiora Cottage. Both these places were in walking distance from each other, I suggest this is how they met. Kenneth's Father, Jack who owned the small caravan park, Dandy Didmont and was an avid member of the Freemasons and could afford to employ the best people in each business.

Following Paulie's birth there was much talk of his natural parent which led to a court case. His Mother simply applied for Child Maintenance, which was rejected. The only reason was because his Mother was given a Solicitor we believed was friends with his Fathers Solicitor who could also have been a Freemason.

Anyway by this point Paulie had a Sister who Kenneth accepts is his child and reassures Celia that everything will be alright. Still no child maintenance and Kenneth deserts both children.

Strange as though it may sound

A couple of years or so soon pass by and Celia is doing well with her two children as a Single Parent. An empty house appears next door to Paulie's and his Family when his Father with a new woman and more children take up this abode. Why would a Father disown his child is one question but would a Father ever assure the release of a Terrorist from prison is another. Throughout Paulie's life he has experienced much trauma. Is it the work Kenneth who has disowned his child or is it just unlucky? Probably just unlucky. Well it started when Paulie was still a young boy. People would call him gay boy for no apparent reason. He would be bullied from an early age and the older he is becoming the wiser to the Scenario he is. He does however follow the trail of an escaped terrorist and persist through his work for Justice.

S.A.S. Unarmed Combat

The One That Got Away (Danny Heffernan) Onward Christian Soldiers

<u>Onward Christian Soldiers.</u>

In his local town, Longtown, Paulie was an avid member of his local church. Saint Michael & all Angels or Arthuret Chuch which stood at the top of a Arthuret hill, which overlooked the town. Paulie took his Christening there after his Birth in 1970. Beyond the Church stood some woodland we call Crow Wood. Both Arthuret Church and Crow Wood were in some 100 meters of each other and many would play in the woods after the weekly Church meetings.

Our local Vicar Mr. Phillips also ran Sunday School from his Vicarage on the Netherby Road. Behind the Vicarage was a small field or Orchard with several fruit trees and about twelve donkeys. Children of Longtown would play on the backs of these donkeys and pick the apples and pairs from the heavily laden fruit trees. Pauls friend Edd Hocking once fell off the back of his donkey with a short sleeved T-Shirt, straight into a bed of strong nettles. Edd later joined the forces and was deployed in Northern Ireland. Paulie was still to receive his orders which eventually came from this his local Church, Arthuret.

Each Easter at this Church youngsters would roll their pace egg down the nearby hill with the aim being the one who rolls the furthest wins. Boy Scouts was also an availability for the locals and they would set tracks in the Crow Wood. Longtown is very much in the Countryside some eight miles North of the closest City, Carlisle. Poachers were in constant search for the biggest kill in fish, pheasants, rabbits and deer. Paulie occasionally joined in this hunt and caught four very big fish with a hand snare. The River Authority had regular encounters with the locals who funded themselves drink tokens with the proceeds. The River Esk flowed steadily through this town with the Armstrongs and the Grahams being two well known Family names. Grahams of the Netherby Estate held Annual Daffodil Sundays for those interested, with a fair and stalls. Young Lochinvar was the legendry young rider of the the Glen who resided here in Longtown. Young Lochinvar made his mark and a large impact on the town with a Housing Estate (Lochinvar Close) and School (Lochinvar Secondary).

Paulie enjoyed his primary years into young adult years in and around this town. Although Paulie was a talented joiner he had several troublesome times in his life which he puts *down to naivety. (Search) The B.I.G.A. picture at www.LuLu.com to learn more of this young Christian Soldiers misadventure. Paulie liked his dogs and would later breed Springer Spaniels keeping his two bitches Jay & Kay.*

Taken to the plot

Paulie was a regular at his local Church and this is where he would take his guidance into the path of an escaped terrorist. Paulie was to travel along the A7 route to Currock in Carlisle, Cumbria. This new house was provided by the local council and the house was next door to the Glaswegian, Danny Heffernan, who was on the run from Police after escaping in a failed bid to do robbery on an ammunition depot. Danny had involvement with the I.R.A. who were intent on blowing up buildings in England. Manchester bombings and Guilford bombings were two tragedies linked to this group. Danny also had Scottish influence with a rough upbringing in the Gorbells of Glasgow. He had a high degree of notoriety up in his

Scottish Lands and was probably chased from Glasgow after he was given a large slash to his jaw. Danny refused to give up his gangland ways and Paulie soon became unwell in Dannys hands. Paulie and his pet Springer Spaniel, Kay had just moved in the new property when Danny started to brandish his weapon at Paulie's door. Kay was barking profusely as Danny waved two daggers in the back garden of their adjoining property. Paulie's Gran followed him on his mission and tried to stop Paulie from getting hurt by this maniac, Danny. Paulie soon found himself a partner who was called Janet. Dannie's absurdity also led him to abuse her and even run his dagger over her private parts. Both Janet and Paulie's Gran died within quick succession and Paulie became suicidal. Daily there was a large bang on the wall, when Danny would order Paulie through to his property. While in his property Danny would show his dagger, threaten Paulie's life and then lead Paulie into sexual abuse. Paulie was living off basic income with his dogs struggling for food and he was at the verge of suicide when Police would take him into psychiatric care for his own safety. Paulie our young Soldier was shaken and stirred by his ordeal but despite attempts from his care team to make Paulie talk, he could say little due to a live threat that he would be killed if he spoke of his ordeal. Four months passed and Paulie had considerable weight loss because of his refusal of meals. Later he was released back to the community and back onto the path of Danny. Although the abuse was still evident Danny had found himself a new partner, a French Girl, Sophie. Danny revealed a newspaper clipping to Paulie, our young Christian (S.A.S) Soldier of Police searching for the Welder who escaped troops on an ammunition depot. Danny revealed that the Welder was him as he had worked on the shipyard as a steel plater and now looking to use Oxygen-Setline on the locked depot. Danny revealed that he had Buckingham Palace in mind and his Cousin who was caught on the scene and arrested while Danny crossed woodland and made his way to Carlisle. This was too much information for Paulie to comprehend and handle so while still under diminished responsibility and state, attacked Danny. Paulie had no option but to talk of his ordeal and produced the One Mind Trilogy which takes Danny's altered ego to be fed to sharks by the Octowarriors. Following this work he produced Angel & Paulie Dee's CLEARER PICTURE to bring out more truths, especially the deaths of his Gran and Girlfriend.

Danny confesses murder

MAYHEM

Paulie was seriously unwell when Danny decided to tell him that he had killed People and Paulie was the top of his next list. Paulie moves house for his own safety as he took all this seriously. Still under psychiatric care

Paulie recollects as much information on the case which he now knows he was guided to for the revealing of his newspaper clipping. There was loss which we are all left helpless but to have a clear understanding of this dangerous criminal, Danny, then it is a loss we are able to accept. Knowing of how dangerous he is and intelligence becoming aware may stop others being seriously abused or maybe killed.

Glaswegian Cockney Riming Slang

Danny was quite well educated though and would excel on T.V.'s Countdown. He would also speak in Cockney Riming Slang...

Apples & Pairs (Stairs)

Dog & Bone (Phone)

Cream Crackered (Shattered)

Pie & Mash (Hash)

Adam and Eve (Believe)

Trouble & Strife (Wife)

Ace of Spades (Aids)

Ruby Murray (Curry)

Barnet Fair (Hair)

Street Fighter (Lighter)

<u>Danny still on the RUN</u>

Paulie disclosed information about Danny with his whereabouts being in Currock. Danny moves home before Police take the case seriously and ten years soon pass. While outside his new local Church (St. Pauls), Danny walked past and Paulie broke out with hysteria and ran into the Church. Paulie shouts to the Warden that a murderer has just walked by and to alert Police. No response so Paulie searches the area and notices a block of flats, named Red Gables, which he links to the Gorbells of Glasgow, (Dannys) home town. Danny brandishes his weapon in Yates Wine Lodge and soon takes over renaming the venue Outrageous (After him I suggest).

<u>Message in Music</u>

Were all Someone's Daughter were all Someone's Son yet we look at each other down the barrel of a Gun. (John Farnham) (The Voice)

He learned how to Steal he learned how to fight. (Elvis Presley) (In the Ghetto)

Paul becomes Successful

The Peace and Prosperity Party on www.YouTube.com

FULL Issue 1 Delusional Dan

In this NEW EDITION of your CLEARER PICTURE we learn of the torment two young teenagers into Adulthood witnessed and experienced. Daniel Heffernan was on the run from Police when he was living next door to Paulie. Danny is also known as the Welder, Highland Beaver, & Jock the Scott. Years passed and so did loved ones when Paulie realized this was the work of Danny who groomed Paulie Dee into sexual activity at knifepoint. Paulie's partner Janet Murray and his Grandmother, Margaret was suspected to have been two of the others of Danny's victims through poisoning with tablets. Danny was a Gangland Rebel or Gangster who had attempted to raid an Army barracks on his mission. It failed but he managed to escape troops. (See) S.A.S. Unarmed Combat (The One that Got Away). Ten years on and his fate beckons. Now believed to be living in the RED GABLES of Chatsworth Square and owning nightclubs and other venues it looks conclusive as he leads night goers to his block or apartment where they could be killed or abused. Originally from the Gorbells which was the roughest upbringing in Scotland was our Danny Boy. Danny's Outrageous is a busy nightclub which has seen many coming and goings and is under his control. He carries weapons and poisons. Paulie Dee has good vision and recognizes truths. His guidance came from the local Churches and Cathedrals which led him to the trail of this escapee which Police are now aware of. Paulie dreamed of Catching criminals and once dreamed of catching Peter Sutcliff the Yorkshire Ripper. He has had his share of tribes and tribulations with others too, including Stuart the Scott and the Bull. He also encounters problems with the Highland Beaver in his rather fascinating first edition of the ONE MIND TRILOGY and celebrated with friends when the Evil Saddam Hussain was hung for his Dictatorship in Kurdish territory of Iraq. Paulie Dee or you may know as Paulie tries to refuse entertaining the bad, but it is sometimes evident, in its extreme. Paulie now Presents PEACE and PROSPERITY and constantly searches for the best solution, this is why he follows in the footsteps of his Mentor with the study of The Delfin Knowledge System. Of course there is good and bad everywhere in Heaven we learn of good and beneficial and in Hell we learn of bad and anger. Which ever way you choose and think of is the way you are destined, but you can change that thought at any given moment. Good advice is given to us all, sometimes to much when all we want to do is let our hair down, few beers and a Kebab. Well my mother told me all in moderation little bad but much good. Leslie Fieger taught me that a positive thought will destroy a negative and light will destroy dark. Focus daily on what you are trying to accomplish. Positive over Negative yet my favorite psychiatrist told me I need to find the balance in much the same way as scales...equal. A little of one should weigh the same as a little of another. Oh it is difficult talking of opposites the next time your out for a drink when the pub is FULL you may see several drunks but you will also see several that is sober. When that drunkard talks to you at the bar you could walk away, but, the bar staff who is sober and beneficial keeps you there for your drink...Cheers. Conspiracy theories are evident on this Planet but so is the meaning of LOVE and Understanding. In This FULL ISSUE 1,2,3,4 & 5 we learn of the full recollection in Paulie Dee's and Angel's lives with much mystery and maybe little understanding.

However it is the attempt for joint Authors to, you know, put the record straight once again. You know the score one step at a time is all were asking, but the question is how far you are willing to go for the TRUTH. The seeds are planted in this EVEN CLEARER PICTURE and follow up to the ONE MIND TRILOGY where we may be left a little wet. Never worry though we are here today, the weather is hot and we will soon dry out. What is this all about you may ask? The purpose of this work concludes ONE jail term and considers three dismissals for YES you guessed CONSPIRACY. Angel who plays her role to the full set out for the truth with Paulie Dee by her side and he helps her come a little closer. Through Hell and High water, YES; but still a little closer. We all need truths, no solution is found in dishonesty. For every problem there must be a solution and in this Full Issue Clearer Picture much is solved but only much. Paulie Dee and Angel do openly talk of what some would call slight errors or mistakes you may know as petty crime but they have been reprimanded for these childhood errors so please feel free in finding forgiveness for both. As you will learn worse things have happened at sea than either of these two would ever dream about, so for this reason focus on forgiveness and understanding of these two very different roles. Danny meets his fate and three are dismissed in order to leave the world a better place for ONE and ALL. We are pleased you are here with us in this EVEN CLEARER PICTURE.

MAYHEM

TODAY's, TOMORROWS and the DAY AFTER's

Full Issue 2

I WANT TO BE A BILLIONAIRE

ON THE FRONT of

Paulie's Magazine

Standing NEXT to

OPRAH and the QUEEN

The FULL Mission

Angel & Paulie Dee's

CLEARER PICTURE

Peace and Prosperity Party

Your No. (1) Subsidiary Party

www.YouTube.com

One Time Start up fee....

Resporation . Immagination . Dedication .

KING KATOOTS LOOT at your favorite www.YouTube.com

One meets his FATE.

Three Dismissals for Conspiracy.

In Order To leave the Planet a better place for All and For One.

Your Ideas and More Ideas www.DELFINGlobal.com

Note: The meek shall inherit the Earth.

MAYHEM

World Exclusive...

Special Edition.

Psychosis into Sane it is the Lord who holds little Blame.

Wonder Drug and National Health TEAM

with Specialists in

Peace...

Love...& Happiness...On a Global Scale you need to hear both side of the TALES.

Silly Little Boys, with their Silly Little Games.

PROFUSIONAL PAULIE...

Our Town Planner Asks for instant dismissal of three Colleagues with NOW six menaces to meet their fate. World of One Awaits.

Angel & Paulie Dee's

CLEARER PICTURE

In this even Clearer Picture we learn of

the results and new goals for both Angel & Paulie Dee and Anneka. In Angel's life she had several Clowns to escape in her bid to be free when she later met Paulie Dee. Angel was born a hermaphrodite in Middlesex and appeared on morning T.V. to announce the youngest ever sex change when still in her teens. She was offered a reward for promoting the News of the World where her story was told but was only ever given a small percentage of the fee for only mentioning it twice until Paulie Dee mentioned it again for her right here in Your Clearer Picture or EVEN CLEARER PICTURE...News of the World. There that's thrice we mentioned it. If I mention it again will you pay us the rest we asked the News of the World. But tell us more and we will think about it, they replied. Angel had not seen Paulie Dee for many years who previously offered her support in her life, but due to psychosis from an outrageous set of ordeals in his own life, he somehow managed to allow for Angel to continue her nightmare. Say it one more time, Angel in this book. Oh YES and that will be Three times I have said it...News of the World. There it was the full story how Angel met Paulie Dee in her local psychiatric hospital. Paulie mentions in his first piece of work. The B.I.G.A. picture project or ONE MIND TRILOGY with a large collection of King Katoots Loot or OctoKash Stash. (FunMun)

Angel, unfortunately was about to develop a drug addiction and started to rely on prostitution to fund her addiction. Paulie set up the Peace and Prosperity Party and became an ideas machine who Society believes runs on Risperidone and other medication while working in the

Personal Development Industry with www.DELFINGlobal.com. This is close, but let us look even closer.

Escape the Clowns

Angel & Paulie Dee had their share to escape. Starting in Middlesex, down to

London and Essex, then back up to Cumbria. My little Cherypie my little baby come home. Paulie was about to shout from the rooftops, come home Angel. Those people we were trying to escape are now in Jail. They are doing a long sentence for all the abuse we went through and we only wanted the truth. The truth it is Paulie Dee. I am an Angel and to be an Angel we need a variety of the collective. One girl that says she is an Angel may have a wicked side, that is all, Paulie or is it Paulie Dee, I see.

Well Angel escaped and decided to tell the

nightmare as it was and could be. Gagged, Raped and Abused were both of our characters...Angel and Paulie Dee. Authorities could do little to support apart from medication and a bit of benefits. These two are living on a whim or pray that is all.

Even Clearer Picture

Paulie Dee was a young soldier

Angel 7 Heaven was a chosen child

Paulie Dee had set out to catch a known terrorist called Daniel Heffernan who had escaped an Army Depot in a bid to gain weapons (SEE) S.A.S. Unarmed Combat. Paulie Dee living on Paul's Planet is widely accepted but on Earth with Angel anything could happen and often did. Yet they are both still young at heart and innocent. Paulie was a victim of some outrageous happenings yet somehow seemed to take the blame for it all. Angel why do you allow me to go through so much suffering. Are you really a chosen child or Hell's Angel Luciphor, did you fall from a Christmas tree or do you light up the sky at night. Angel you were born hermaphrodite had a sex change, entered prostitution and took heroin. Paulie Dee is worried about you, Angel and he says you are on your way to Hell when you should take your followers with you. What followers are they asked Angel. Peter Sutcliffe killed prostitutes in Yorkshire in the mid eighties and Angel was nearing the start of a new nightmare. There was so many being murdered that Marshall Cavendish released some of the Casebooks. Paulie was hot on the heals of this escaped terrorist who had moved into the area. Society was shaking when Paulie suggests NOT to get *caught up with this movie where you think that it is all real. It is real said "Angel" It is only real when your mind tells you it is, replies Paulie.*

MAYHEM

Clearer Picture

Angel goes to Hell and dances with the Devil. Well Angel now you are here with your Merry men...Peter and Danny, Angel you can leave now. You are NOT the fallen Angel. You are one of God's Children...the chosen child. Leave NOW...Heaven awaits for now you need Earth.

Angel returns from Hell to Earth

Peter and Danny are down there Paulie with Luciphor and guess what so is

Saddam Hussein. He said I should come back to your Earth, Paulie while I await Heaven. Angel your nightmare....it has stopped. How has it stopped Paulie my drug addiction is still there. Drug addiction, Angel we are all addicts. Caffeine, Nicotine and Alcohol you can buy freely. Who decides what drugs you should have if you can afford them. You hurt nobody my little Cherry Pie so why do they hurt you. We hurt nobody yet others try to hurt us said Paulie Dee

Jealousy, Hate, Anger and Frustration runs rampant and we need to replace this with LOVE...HAPPINESS...PEACE and PROSPERITY

The No 1 Ideas Machine Paulie Dee U Cee

1 The Delfin Knowledge System

(Leslie Fieger) Mentor. (Paul Dickinson) Promoter

2 The One Mind Trilogy

(Paul Dickinson)

3 Holy Bible

Believers.Kings.Queens .God and Saint Paul

4 King Katoots Loot

(Paul Dickinson)

5 Peace and Prosperity Party

(Paul Nigel DicKinGson)

6 Music Millionaire

(Paul Dickinson)

7 Mini Moose

(Paul Dickinson)

8 Octowarriors

(Paul Dickinson)

9 999 Doctors Liason Line

(Paul Nigel Dickinson)

10 PaulNigel 10 with 10 out of 10

(Paul, Paulie Dee, God, My Creator)

For further talks about ideas or inventions

e-mail: PaulieDee80@yahoo.com

The Clearer Picture continued...Paulie Dee met the Three Kings with his Angel

Governments were outraged when they found all that Paulie Dee and Angel were trying to do was resolve situations while taking as much responsibility for their own lives as possible.

The same Government which think they can control you with cash, work and zealousy.

The TAX Man in Britain alone could give

every person £100,000 and NOT Miss a penny. Paper and ink is not so expensive and we have realms at our prints NOW. It is OK though as a system or matrix we only see another virtual array of Color, Light and Intelligence and although it may seem like reality. The only real thing is Spirit which possesses the Power to Think. I mean what have we...Fancy cars, Boats, Airplanes, Superheroes, Helicopters, Sky, Sand and Snowflakes...we have it all. We also have...God. Jesus. Queen. King. Mother. Father. Worker. Colleague. Armies.

Peace. Love. Happiness. Resentment.

Why only some good?

It is All GOOD is it NOT Why Resentment.

Why Resentment

Simply because of the two poles in much the same way as a battery.

Positive Charge and Negative Charge.

We think we are achieving so much yet wake up to find that all we have done is taken a small step.

Do NOT be so disheartened though you can be good but also little bad.

How can we understand LIGHT without DARK.

Paulie Dee arrives at the Hospital

After entering the back of a Police van at a Doctors Surgery and banging his head on the door while trying to climb in, we set off for the Psychiatric Hospital for review. No Admission and turned away, was to be, but how when I Love them here. Were they thinking of what was best for me or not caring. Again we have the two sides. I could have enjoyed some respite but the walk home was intriguing. Do they repel or attract YES two opposites attract yet Like also Attracts Like in Similarity. We are drawn with LOVE. We are all very much alike, but yet unique and different. The two poles forming equilibrium.

Angel feeds the No1 Ideas Machine Chocolate.

Angel you have give me an idea if I mention that newspaper one more time they may advertise with us.

Well I will mention it 3 times

"My NAME is Paulie Dee"

I have a few good ideas you see.

From Chocolate Mini Moose,

To a Gold Guitar for 100 BAR,

Poundland was a pound which soon became £1,000 yet,

Mums shop at Iceland.

Dads they know best,

but trust me I have the rest,

an Idea you see.

Because I am an idea you see.

My name is Paulie Dee.

Ten more Top Ideas 2 Cee

PND Shows and Seminars in association with Heathers Heather's (Fresh Fruit & Florist) and Plain Jane's (Bridal and Wedding Wear) Oh its good.

Cheep Chario (Everything £10.00)

Gold Guitar 100 BAR (Everything £100.00)

Grand Demand (£1,000; £10,000; £100,000) Showrooms

T.V. Shows

1. Born No.1 (Athletics) (Football) (Pop Star) etcetera.

2. Wild Cats (Inside view of Females Prison)

3. Wipe the Floor with Angel and Paulie Dee (Card Game) Versus Authorities.

4. Risk it for a Biscuit (Well would YOU)

5. Dance for the world (Europe, Asia, Africa, Australasia and America)

6. Music Millionaire (Pop & Music questions)

Yes... I will mention that paper for you Angel I know you are friends with Max Clifford. News of the World for all Sport, News and Television. News of the World...On the world.

Angel took away the wrapper of his GOLD BAR and the ideas machine kept his calm but was still churning. With modern technology we are in a good position to work from home on a sensible basis. I personally write, write and write with sometimes little sleep, but find contentment with www.DELFINGlobal.com.

Fancy writing and publishing...well you can at www.LuLu.com Paulie Dee, cried Angel, I have taken Danny Heffernan and Peter Sutcliff out of the game I am sure the Bull who was blocked and Stuart the Scott are next.

Try your games with King Katoots Loot or OctoKash Stash (FunMun) try to WIN the most with your favorite card or board or party game.

(Search) King Katoots Loot

www.YouTube.com

(part of the PaulNigel10 collection).

Is this The End...Or Beginning of the End.

Better Now...

It will all get better in time (Leona Lewis)

What more do you need to know.

www.DELFINGlobal.com

Hi Paulie, it's the Octowarriors, what's

happening with Stuart the Scott and the Bull? Well you see Stuart is a sex case who raped and took Angel into Prostitution and Heroin. He also assaults and caused great commotion in others lives. The Bull, well you see he assaulted me while talking to a man in a wheelchair and then pushed my meal out my hand. Oh leave them to us Paulie Dee...Angel is right they will go into the Pashacarts to be fed to those hungry sharks by us Octowarriors and the Conspiracy Crew. The world is FREE and so are you.

P.S. Don't have nightmares the Authorities are here with us.

If you are mentioned in any of our work we thank YOU for your trust. We are here for you always. Profits from this work will go to those mentioned both within... The B.I.G.A. picture and the CLEARER PICTURE with Angel and Paulie Dee, who match our integrity.

<u>CONCLUSIONS & ONLY EXCLUSIONS</u>.

Danny Heffernan (Terrorism)(Murder)(Rape)(Gangland & other Gangster Outrageous Crimes)

Peter Sutcliff (Serial Murderer)

Stuart the Scott (Rapist)

The Bull who was Blocked (Defielded)

The Highland Beaver (Shark infested waters with Octowarriors)

&

Saddam Hussein

(Hung) for Killing Kurds and Genocide.

The ROAD to HELL is paved with GOOD Intentions (Have FUN) those Six. You HAVE the Choice GOOD versus Evil. Common Sense prevails. Good luck on Your FULL Mission Transforming the way the World thinks One Person and One Person at a time starting with you.

www.DELFINGlobal.com

Together... We Achieve More.

The Ideas Machine churns on and could this one be for YOU...A Sister or Brother Magazine for the BIG Issue called the FULL Issue.

Sorry Seems to be the Hardest Word but only when your NOT.

Guess What I'm *** Coz I've done nothing. (Nothing) Innocent until proven Guilty.

Paulie Dee and Angel are innocent. Take them others away States the Demon Judges.

(One Mind Trilogy)

Author of the One Mind Trilogy

States (Total Fascination)

Good night

God Bless

Sleep tight.

Oh I could go on and on but keep a look out for my next work...World Case Scenario

(CAPTURED).

An idea Especially for Toys R Us...

Special Gifts R Us and Octowarriors R Us www.YouTube.com

Mini Moose for Disneyworld.

Other ideas open on a profit share scheme (Includes all). The Peace and Prosperity Party would accept 24/7 Opening hours for all known stockists, street traders, wholesale or Supermarkets so long as Alcohol closes at midnight. Good luck...Your Going Places with a Real Deal. Thanks to Gloria Hunniford and David Dickinson.

Blessings to you all.

Log on today... tomorrow we have our hay or (OctoKash) FunMun by the Million and Billion. You say you want a leader but you can't seem to make up your mind were the lyrics of which *famous Popstar from Minneolapasis...like many. Long live the Prince.*

I say Goodbye to...

Les Fumes (Lettings Manager) (McFlights Housing & Sons)

Patricia White (Housing Benefit)

including...Andy from our Local Employment and Benefits Department. Department of Social Security. D.H.S.S. You know National Insurance Number and hard to get an appointment. Well Andy you are just to handy now take that grin of your face. Pick it up at the door your UB40. All three dismissals for Conspiracy to make Paulie Dee homeless and broke.

And for the REST of us enjoy your favorite Red Red Wine UB40.

Jesus Loves...Jesus Saves...Jesus is Your Saviour and we are here on Gods Planet with (Total Fascination). Coming Soon and exclusive to www.YouTube.com

Moroccan Holidays

TrueBluesCUFC

PaulNigel10

(Faith Formula)

FORGIVENESS...FOOLISHNESS...FLAWLESNESS

Fortune.......Favors......Bravery

Has the equivalence of LIFE for all.

Just Ask Albert. This is it though from the No1 ide machine, one for the road, a Special Edition of Mr Mrs hosted by NONE Other than Peter and Jorda with Peter deciding the category of Relationships given three categories.

Mrs.£$Money

Mrs.??? Big Question

Mrs.Naughty but Nice

Booby prize a Cream Cake

Star Prize £$£ Money

The BIG QUESTION 'R' We Still Together

The choice is Clear

The choice is Clearer Picture.

Yours Truly Angel & Paulie Dee

On a Planet somewhere near YOU.

No further Questions.

You may leave the Courtroom.

Work dedicated for Jordan and Lucy with their Special Crew...THE FULL MISSION.

Why NOT tell us your Story for the NEXT

FULL MISSION in Paulie's Magazine

Special mentions to.....

PAUL on Paulie's Planet.

Long LIVE the King and his Son

Prince Paulie Dee,

Angel, Oprah Winfrey, & the Queen,

WITH YOU & ME.

Well is that it Paulie Dee asked Angel

You know this ideas machine/thing is still runnin after eating more chocolate...Oh it was the taste o Paradise. This is it and I am going.

For 16+'s to Study...

Delusions . Profusions . Conclusions

While listening to the Delfin Knowledge System a planning business ideas.

Linking...PND Shows & Seminars to

Paul Nigel DicKinGson

PersoNal Development

AND

Post Natal Depression

With

Police Northern Department

www.DELFINGlobal.com

Today's, Tomorrow's & the Day After's Full Issue 3

THE EVEN CLEARER PICTURE

(Psychiatric Services)

Dr. Muller

Dr. Barlow

&

Dr. Nair

FULL MISSION 3

Three Doctors

Here we have a Grand man in a psychotic state after years of abuse and torture at the hands of a known Terrorist who had escaped on foot from an attempt to raid an Army Barracks with Buckingham Palace in mind. After threatening Paulie with his life he sexually abused him and his partner, who was later found dead. Paulie or Paulie Dee as we know him wrote a Collection of books to explain the trauma, but still people were unsure. This leads us to The Even Clearer Picture following The One Mind Trilogy & S.A.S. Unarmed Combat (The One that got away). Daniel Heffernan and The Full Mission or Full Issue was to secure his arrest. Welcome to an even Fuller Issue of the Even Clearer Picture right here in Full Issue 3. Paulie was a joiner for many years and loved football, fishing and much other sport. He has tried boxing, Karate and can run 100 meters in 10.00 seconds sometimes. He is fit, he walks for *miles, has owned a small joinery business called Rosewood Joinery and generally accomplished much in life. He has two wonderful children Jordan and Lucy, he doesn't say much about his third, his love child from the Woman's Hostel but wishes him well.*

He joined in DELFIN's Mission "transforming the way the world thinks one person one mind at a time" in 1997

So why does he need three top Doctors.

Paulie moved into a property at Marina Crescent and Daniel already lived at Marina Crescent with only a partition wall and garden gate separating them. Paulie witnessed some scary times here being pinned to a wall with a dagger, then seeing it ran over his Girlfriends private parts, his Grandmother passed away, his dogs had to go to care (who were beautiful black and white Spaniels called Jay and Kay. Paulie became suicidal and looked for an easy solution. The abuse was ongoing and Janet (God Bless her Sole) passed away but left valuable clues about her killer she had named her Son Jordan as Dan the Man abused her and she was found dead, later with a suicide set up. Was this Daniel or did she opt for her solution to take her from the misery she suffered with Daniel. Paulie was taken back into care when he fell in love with Victoria and later married her. They had a child together they named Lucy but later had to take a bow and settle for divorce after Victoria hit him over the head with a wine bottle, spat in his face and slept with his friends. She later played on Paulie's psychosis through the Courts to stop any contact and tries to delude authorities that Paulie is dangerous. Yes he was diagnosed with schizophrenia but the voice he hears is the one of God and thinks he is his Son. Not all strains of psychosis is dangerous or alarming in fact some people find Full recovery and Paulie is very close. Careful monitoring and prescription medication works well in his life and here he is explaining to the world in Your

Even Clearer Picture. With his Son adopted in 2001 while on remand for assault, two Doctors had the opportunity to meet Paulie where he was given the opportunity to explain his side of events. At first the psychosis looked incurable with Grandiose Ideas thoughts of Self Harm and Suicide and was under the impression that people were out to kill him, which we now realize he was talking about Daniel his next door neighbor who told Paulie he had killed before with Paulie top of his next list.

Very scary times and Paulie was given Intensive Care with 24 hr supervision in Carleton Clinic.

Trying to opt for euthanasia and thinking so many times of killing himself Doctors were left with little alternative to place him on anti-psychotic medication which he eventually accepted. His care team has done a tremendous job working with him in the Community and is recognized as a success story. He remembers to keep regular appointments with his latest and maybe final Doctor who Paulie calls a top Doc...Dr. Nair.

Dr. Nair asks Paulie a Question

Are you still receiving psychic slaps or blows. Paulie responds...No that was a one off when Kazza was round showing me tai-chi. Kazza, Paulie who is he. He is my friend Dr. Nair who does Yoga and studies other PersoNal Development material. It is alright now and he has introduced me to his Cousin who I offer the World to on www.YouTube.com The Girl who was Offered the World.

So Paulie, every cloud has a Silver lining.

YES this is obvious we have a beginning and an end we are all going through the process of life.

If the bubble bursts blow a new one.

The Planet was dark and almost looked as if we were condemned, do you remember telling me this Paulie.

YES with all the War and Terrorism I said the

world would be condemned this is why I set up a Subsidiary Party on YouTube called The Peace and Prosperity Party with two things on our mind...PEACE & PROSPERITY. With links to www.DELFINGlobal.com this is a must see video and people did comment on the psychological affect this Party would play. You must go back on the ward now your dinner is served. Paulie constantly talks of two sides...left and right, male and female, light and dark, up and down, good and evil, positive and negative, suicide and euphoria and so on. Here he is in a psychiatric hospital with diverse cultures and backgrounds, slight disturbances from some people YET Paul remembers his Please and Thank yous and seems to be enjoying himself. Unbelievable...he sings, dances and attends church meetings, meditation classes and shows off his karate ability at some BIG BOYS. He is a Gift with a GIFT he calls the Delfin Knowledge System which more and more are becoming aware of because of him.

Paulie asks Dr. Nair the Question...what is your FULL MISSION

Well Paulie I was born far away and come here to the Clinic to complete my training as psychiatrist along with my team. I heard about you Paulie and really thought I could help with your case and as you know I have done exactly that. I agree with you about your Religion that Christians and Muslims should unite.

GOOD LUCK with your work and the ARREST of Daniel, Paulie.

Paulie asks Dr. Barlow what is your FULL MISSION

You know Paulie I work at a very different

hospital from the Carleton Clinic and I was

surprised to find you hear. Nevertheless YOU are well on the road to recovery, keep taking your meds and stay clear from trouble and any form of violence. It is well to avoid bullies and troublemakers keep in touch with the

Assertive Outreach.

Congratulations Paulie transformation is always at work.

<u>Paulie asks Dr. Muller the same Question what is your FULL MISSION</u>

My Mission is big Paulie but like yours achievable. Good luck with your case which includes the Arrest of Daniel Heffernan and the reunion with your children some day. Paul I will miss you and thank you for being so honest and reliable at every point even when you wanted a way out. You now understand to find the balance between Positive and Negative. Good LUCK Paulie and Well Done.

Of course Doctors and other service professions have a Larger than Life Mission and they do their very best sometimes with a bad bunch.

Some others of course are usually given another chance and this one is for YOU Paulie.

Paulie thanks his team

Respect to you all including Colin, Aiden and Leslie.

Dallan, Phyllis, Ann, Jo, All other nursing staff who have met him.

Special thanks...my psychiatrist Dr. Nair.

My favorite psychiatrist Dr. Muller and thanks to Dr. Barlow. There are of course other Doctors who I give a mention to on my TABLETS (Which Ones Help You Most) video on www.YouTube.com

Is this the End of a particular terrifying ordeal for ANGEL & PAULIE DEE or the beginning of a new nightmare.

The way things are going it looks like the beginning of a new nightmare but the light still shines. It is NOT over until the FAT GIRL SINGS.

Suggested diet Fish, Fruit and Veg with small amounts of meat & Sticky Toffee Pudding.

There you go Piece of Cake.

www.DELFINGlobal.com

or

www.LeslieFieger.com

Any Ideas for us said the Doctors. Yes said our No1 Ideas Machine a T.V show called Messing with Marbles (an inside view to a Psychiatric Hospital.

Yes it is Unique not many witness our views. There is all sorts of ups and downs in these places.

Today's, Tomorrow's & the Day After's Full Issue 4

JOCK the SCOT

YOUR No 1 Subsidiary Party

PEACE & PROSPERITY PARTY

www.YouTube.com

Jock the Scot was determined to do damage and he had six people on his hit list. Darrell Smilth and Davie Fullins. You are in Full Issue 4 Jock are you sure you need six. What about Eckster & John Sprocket he said. You have to stop this killing said Paulie. Those are the four I really wanted he said . Well Darrell robbed my Grandmother so I give him a beating but he still continues with his stupidity. It has gone on so long I feel like putting a bullet in his head. Davie Fullins I just want to beat to death. Eckster and John Sprocket can rot. Jock there day's are numbered can you think how you would really like to spend your time. I am a builder he says. I have built myself a property, do you want to see. You are the Leader of the Peace and Prosperity Party why do you mention Eckster and John Sprocket. Well Eckster punched my teeth out and John Sprocket kicked a glass into my friends eye. I later went on to You Bet with this friend, Jimmy and he was answering questions about his favorite pop star, Prince who he says is a lyrical master. Like you said in Full Issue 1,2 & 3 there is good and bad everywhere we have positive and negative. Is this the Full Issue 4 or Full Mission 4? asks Jock. Either one was the response. Well I can think of at least two more for my hit list with Timmy Ball and Sam Spith but they are probably best left to the Octowarriors (Search) Octowarriors R Us on www.YouTube.com.

Well that's my six said Jock the Scott that is all you will allow is it not. Yes that is all in this Full Issue 4 or Full Mission 4 but tell me a little more you know about your dreams, hopes and aspirations. What is it you would like to achieve. Peace and Prosperity but what else. Jock the Scott did of course have ambition he has already built himself a house. He would like Gold bath taps and accessories, a helicopter and to see his child do well at School and in life. Angel arrives but refuses to Dance with the devil even just one more time which would take these six straight into Hell. Paulie Dee what do you think? Well that is certainly where they deserve to be. Jock the Scott grins, Angel you do not have to dance with him any more to take them there, I have a big Van, that will take them there with the Octowarriors. Jock was of course some form of hit man and very annoyed. Jock, Jock, Jock you've done it, here are the Octowarriors with their Pashacarts who will take them to be fed to sharks.

John Bellmont & Duncan (Shell Garage)
Victoria Stowell (Witchcraft)

Also found guilty of conspiracy sentencing awaits.Full Issue 1,2,3 & 4 The Clearer Picture was produced in order to leave the world a better place for ONE and All.

The meek shall inherit the Earth.

Thank you.

www.DelfinGlobal.com

The Six in total who were found Guilty of Conspiracy were ordered to do 200 hours of unpaid work on the Octowarriors Pashacarts.

Like we say...

It is Not over untill the Fat Girl Sings

Is that Michele Mc Manis I hear.

Nearly The End. To Appear in Full Issue 5 or Full Mission 5 (FIVE is ALIVE)

e-mail: pndevelopments@hotmail.co.uk.

Todays, Tomorrows & the Day Afters
Full Mission 5 FIVE IS ALIVE

Angel, Paulie Dee and the Three Kings were reflecting on this story and thought what if you could rid the world of 6 prolific criminals, 6 bullies or vagabonds and 6 who have had conspiracy in your life, make your list now.

MAYHEM

List 6 Prolific Criminals...

1)

2)

3)

4)

5)

6)

List 6 Bullies or Vagabonds...

1)

2)

3)

4)

5)

6)

And

6 who have Conspiracy over YOU...

1)

2)

3)

4)

5)

6)

Leaving a clear path of your top ten ideas...

1)

2)

3)

4)

5)

6)

7)

8)

9)

10)

Full Mission 1,2,3,4 & 5 or Full Issue 1,2,3,4 & 5

Became SERIOUS ISSUE 1

Daniel Heffernan (The Highland Beaver) Stuart the Scott and the Bull were due arrest. Saddam Hussain is hung and Peter Sutcliff given Life to mean Life behind bars. Jock the Scott finishes the six bullies and six serve 200 hours unpaid work for conspiracy. Special thanks to the three Doctors, Angel and the Three Kings with Paulie Dee.

Google search....World News PaulNigel10

Google search....Angel Paris Jordan

Angel & Paulie Dee's (Clearer Picture)

This is of course SERIUOS ISSUE 1 and

Danny Heffernan is about to be...Arrested and

Charged with Terrorism, Murder and Rape.
P.S. Don't have nightmares GOD is LOVE.
Your life and destiny is in your control...refuse to entertain that which serves against You and focus entirely on the BENEFICIAL and PURPOSFULL.

Serious Issue 1

SIX Await HELL

1 Arrest imminent (Danny Heffernan)

Alias...Jock the Scott or the Welder

2 Life Sentence (Peter Sutcliff)

3 Death Penalty (Sadam Hussein)

4 Stuart the Scott

5 The Bull

6 the Highland Beaver

Delusion...Danny (BOY) Heffernan

Profusion...Carry the world before YOU

Conclusion...If YOU can't be GOOD be Careful

Hope you enjoyed your read.

DicKinGson's Palace

Proudly Presents ... P. N. Developments

Millions & Billions of OctoKash

To be WON with

Your One Mind Trilogy

NOW £240.00 with FREE (48) piece OctoKash and Case

STASH 1 (Value) £39.95 (16) piece

STASH 2 (Value) £84.95 (32) piece

STASH 3 (Value) £149.95 (48) piece

Search...King Katoots Loot

@ www.YouTube.com

Search...The B.I.G.A. picture (One Mind Trilogy)

@ www.LuLu.com

Sponsored by

www.DELFINGlobal.com

666 is the number of the BEAST or the DEVIL in our work. In Angel & Paulie Dee's CLEARER PICTURE we manage to take at least one group of six back to Hell. Jock the Scott took out the six bullies. We were left with six on the Pashacarts feeding Sharks the bodies of twelve with the help of the Octowarriors. The Devils plot is weakened and GOD is STRONG. With this work we take away the BAD to make way for the GOOD. Destroy DARK with LIGHT and find the balance between Positive and Negative, Male and Female, Left and Right, Up and Down. Harmony and Bliss, Peace and Prosperity. But most of all we have JUSTICE

Good conquers Evil

Good Luck from

Angel 7 Heaven & Prince Paulie Dee

The Ultimate Conclusion.

There is danger in most walks of Society and many do NOT even know the friends they are with. Danny was DELUDED to think that he could become a notorious criminal by making attempts to gain weapons with a certain Palace in mind. Danny obviously had set his target to high and his attempt failed. He would NOT give up though and made his mark with Gangsters and holds the scars from Gorbells Gangland Days. Most probably chased from Glasgow and arriving in Carlisle he lives in the same community as Paulie, Janet and Paulie's Gran. Using blades and strong tablets he sees off Paulie's Gran and Janet while abusing Paulie sexually. Still intent on his notoriousness with a certain life of crime he moves to the town centre. Gaining money from his many Victims he takes over his favorite Venues and renames them OUTRAGEOUS and Little Frankies where he meets his next Victims. Paul obviously has Profusions in the way of carrying the world before him but the abuse by Danny left him a little sidetracked on his DELFIN Mission. Profusion will always be there though and his ideas reignite with ideas for television shows and shops. He is about to hear of the arrest of Deluded Dan and the saga continues, but Profusion Paulie comes to this Conclusion...The work of the Devil is evident on Gods Planet, we have Bad as well as Good, we have Light as well as Dark. We have all heard that we will meet our maker ONE day...for Danny he will be dark. If you are like most people you will find forgiveness for Angel & Paulie Dee our stars in this product but would allow Danny to go to HELL. It has been suggested at my local Church and Cathedral that Good will overcome Evil and steps have been taken. Police have an extremely difficult time with Notorious Criminals with our Justice System having a limited time for them to be released back into the community. You guessed for most to re-offend, my prayers are with you. For Good to prevail we all need to focus on the Positive Beneficial walk of life and refuse to entertain the Negativity.

GOD is GOOD and GOD is LIGHT

Think thoughts of Peace and Think thoughts of Prosperity.

Be Loving, Lovable and Loved.

Be Happy, Healthy and Wealthy.

Angel & Paulie Dee's CLEARER PICTURE

Serious Issue 1....concludes with the Arrest of Daniel Heffernan.

Look out for my next work where Daniel will be tried before a Jury with Treason, Terrorism, Murder & Rape. This work is planned to be called World Case Scenario (CAPTURED) and will give extensive insight into the seriously Deluded Dan.

All is well that ends well...

Good Luck in your future.

King Katoots Loot or OctoKash can be used with

Any Board, Card or Domino game.

A,B,C,DicKinGson's Games Incorporated.

(c) Copyright P. N. Dickinson 2010

(The Incredible)

Angel & Paulie Dee's

CLEARER PICTURE...

FULL MISSION (If a Job is worth doing it is worth doing right)

THE FULL MISSION Angel and Paulie Dee's CLEARER PICTURE

Is brought to you as a World Exclusive.

www.DELFINGlobal.com

www.LuLu.com

www.YouTube.com

For subsequent copies of Angel & Paulie Dee's (Clearer Picture) or

King Katoots Loot (Ideal for Any Board, Card or Domino Game)

e-mail: pndevelopments@hotmail.co.uk

Make YOUR own Great Minds Think Alike (ARRESTED) with two Clearer Pictures an A3 Foldio and GREAT MINDS THINK ALIKE (ARRESTED)

Sitting on the Fence

You may have heard the phrase before, in fact you have been guilty of this in your life, sitting on the fence. It is a saying for those who can't make up their mind. Through my previous work you will see that Angel and Paulie Dee avoid doing this and bring an escaped Terrorist to Justice. Paulie has a friend called Kazza who has done exactly that, sitting on the fence. Of no ordinary fence I may add. The fence he sat on was the Palace wall while in a drunk state and checking security. Over my life I have heard numerous incidents surrounding the Royal Family and I now believe that people should leave them alone and NOT put so much pressure on them. The I.R.A in Serious Issue 1 and now Kazza in Serious Issue 2. Coming down from the fence is sometimes difficult but I am down and believe that it is the Government who is causing disputes and corruption NOT the Royal Family. Paulie was abused in the hands of a Terrorist and took a good hiding with the use of Tai-Chi by Kazza, is it for sticking up for the Royals, I wonder? To be punished in the hands of a Terrorist is a BIG ISSUE and SERIOUS ISSUE. To take a telling by the use of Tai-Chi and then retaliate in the way of Karate is totally a different entity but still uncalled for. I mean what have the Royals done wrong apart from giving power to a Government who do the day to day running of the Economics of our Country. The Queen also gives us public a privilege of voting for a Political Party who makes the decisions. I am sure you are aware of the War on Terrorism it was George Bush and Tony Blair who ordered this NOT the Royal Family. The I.R.A. of which has coverage in Serious Issue 1 with the Arrest of Danny, who may have been a ringleader and now here in your Serious Issue 2 where we find a man sitting on the fence. There is a difference though but still focusing his energy on who he blames. The only person we have to blame for the way of our world is ourselves, if we could do better, then we should. I am NOT into pointing the finger but some are, others are left on the fence, but I choose Unity. On the Internet we have the Global Government who are standing for Peace and Prosperity on a Global Scale, check it out on www.YouTube.com. The current local Government are in the habit of taking your money and spending it on the things they think worthwhile. Renovation and Improvement are their contributories at your expense. You could argue that some money is wasted but who has not wasted money, again if you could do any better then you should. Blaming others is giving away power. Accept responsibility for where we find ourselves and keep focussed on what it is that we are looking for, in my case Peace and Prosperity which I will achieve. Good luck to those who count themselves Monarchs it is nothing for us to be envious or jealous about, they are just like me and you.

What do you make of it Angel asks Paulie Dee. Well I am NOT sitting on the fence but Kazza seems harmless by doing so, yet wonder why. He says he was checking security Angel, but how absurd, he was drunk. Well what have the Royals done to upset these people asks Angel. Nothing replies Paulie Dee they just look for publicity. You know Angel there are NOT many who are as innocent as us as we take on this debate, let us get it right from the start, NO sitting on the fence. LOVE or HATE we have to decide. LOVE to LOVE, Peace and Prosperity, there I don't sit on the shelf or fence, why do that.

Not Another Section

Now remember Paulie Dee (Peace and Prosperity) with his Angel. Kazza shows up and another section hangs overhead. More lockup for the innocent. Leaving Danny and Kazza on the out.

Look....Kazza and Danny (Destructive)

Paulie Dee (Constructive)

Authorities (Decision Maker)

Why section Paulie Dee to leave these looking supreme, taking constructiveness and leaving destructiveness is quite dangerous as we found in World Case Scenario (CAPTURED) at www.LuLu.com.

As for the decision maker it was probably a difficult decision, but will they ever see the difference between LIGHT and DARK, this is the purpose of my work.

Come down from the fence, stand for your rights, but remember Light has more POWER than DARK. When we press that button on our torch, we have light from energy. When we press that button again to turn off that torch we have no power or dark. It is simple to be dark but it has no power. Light is what takes the power and power begets power. We are in a constant state of growth with Light, that is power and constructive. The opposite states Dark and Destructive.

Peace and Prosperity did of course prevail and Justice is a foregone conclusion. We are on GODS Planet, who did you think would WIN, GOOD over EVIL of course.

Paulie Dee was soon released back into the Community after explaining Peace and explaining Prosperity.

(Search) TheWorldInHisHands at www.YouTube.com for full meaning of Peace and Prosperity see just where we are at on achieving this mission. (Globally or Individually)

Peace and Prosperity is achievable and some already have it, it will WIN.

As in Serious Issue 1 we remember the Good while eliminating the bad... my Name is Paulie Dee

(I have a few more)

GOOD Ideas 2 Cee.

1) Mr Whippy Ice cream fruity filler

   (Cherry, Chocolate Sauce and Mint Chip)

2) Miracle Oil (Mixture) Coconut Oil, Honey, Argon Oil, Saffron flavoured with fruit or cinnamon (Oral)

3) Under One Roof (Cheapest in) Gas, Electric, Phone, Internet packages and Home Improvement.

4) (OTB) Outside of the Box for all Personal Development needs including Mind, Body and Spirit.

5) FunMun or KidsKash (OctoKash) Stash

   King Katoots Loot www.YouTube.com

6) www.DELFINGlobal.com & www.LeslieFieger.com

Order of the Highest Power

Now you will be aware from Angel & Paulie Dee's CLEARER Picture that our Monarchy has been under threat. We have those who believe in this and those who do NOT. The facts are we are in no position to argue it is what it is. The Royal Family is the most famous family, arguably on our Planet. This is why they have so much attention with press and T.V. and other literature.

Some people send the Queen presents others try to give threat.

The Serious Issue is this....The I.R.A. dislike and blame them but plenty LOVE our Royals, I will say and suspect innocence. Each individual has the same opportunity on our Planet, if you want a Palace build one, if you want to be in control of your own life and destiny then jump down off that fence and search our web-sites for more information.

On a personal level, I see it as the Government who makes the decisions and NOT the Royal Family. It is mistake to blame the Royals for our world...remember this is God's Planet and he has given man free will. You choose your own success and let others choose theirs. If the transaction benefits all concerned it will go ahead. I am off the fence and say that anything it is which so ever ye desire, pray to receive them and you will have them or that thing.

Paulie has released numerous books...The B.I.G.A. picture collection or One Mind Trilogy...The Clearer picture or Great Minds Think Alike (ARRESTED) and Onward Christian Soldiers S.A.S Unarmed Combat all available from www.LuLu.com.

Each book he wrote brought him a little closer to the truth and gave him a B.I.G.A. Clearer picture and he still wonders if his Father has had Conspiracy over his life.

In the book S.A.S Unarmed Combat we learn that Paulie was guided to the plot where he eventually brought an escaped terrorist to JUSTICE. Could this Terrorist have been let out of prison for the reason of persecuting Paulie and Paulie was placed strategically next door to him.

We already know that Solicitors have had involvement with the Freemasons could the Doctors also be involved with this set up. Danny and Liam Heffernan tried to raid an Army Barracks or Weapons Base and were foiled. Liam Heffernan is still behind bars for this but Danny has yet to serve his sentence. Did Military Police actually catch all at the scene and it was a Masonic set up which allowed Danny back on the street or is the truths more likely that which was revealed through Paulie's previous work, (S.A.S) Unarmed Combat

It does state in a Bible which I have read that you should hate your Son and hate your Wife but love the Lord yet to take things to the extreme of Conspiracy against your Son is NOT mentioned. Biblical teaching learns us of Forgiveness and if the Conspiracy theory is true I would still forgive in the Name of Jesus Christ but many will never. All I need is truths.

Never an Angel

Paul has only met one Angel, Angel Paris Jordan and she used heroin and prostitution. Paul has confessed to petty crime which he REPENTS. He was also reprimanded through the courts for his childhood stupidity and firmly believes himself to be on the right path after years of study within the Personal Development Industry (PDI).

We are born to sin to be forgiven in the Name of Jesus Christ, start to REPENT your Sin, now.

No matter what mistakes we make the only people who should be able to punish us are our parents when we are children and the court of LAW as we grow older.

Danny showed Paulie a News Paper clipping saying he was a Terrorist and Danny also said he had been in prison when he cut an inmate under his nose, then made him drink his own blood. The truth always comes out and there is no smoke without fire, for me this could have been Conspiracy from my Father, but Onward Christian Soldiers (S.A.S) Unarmed

Combat suggests Paulie took his guidance through the Church and from God to re-secure Danny's arrest.

Terrorists should never be let out of prison to take away years of Policing but the same thing has happened recently with Peace talks through Jerry Adams to re-release approx sixty suspected I.R.A. members.

Now it is only Conspiracy but there is an element of truth and none of dishonesty. They have arrested me more times than Danny yet it is him who is a Terrorist and me who is the leader of the subsidiary Party...The Peace and Prosperity Party. www.YouTube.com

I have asked for Criminal Injuries to pay me out for what I had to go through with Danny but was refused. I became suicidal and was taken into a Mental Health Hospital and guess what they told me the best way to go about it.

They also told my ex-partner the same, how to commit the act of suicide. Most think better of it and live to tell the tale others are less fortunate. Of course Doctors could be part of Conspiracy so could Solicitors. A Masonic set up is unprovable but my Father who disowned me proves my very point (There could be wrong decisions).

I did recover from what I went through though and went on to have two beautiful children who I have NOT seen for many years, more Conspiracy again from Doctors and Solicitors (MASONS) maybe.

I guess I was unlucky being a Masons Son but I live on.

Confusion YES Why should a Doctor hurt somebody, they are meant to heal you are they NOT. Why should your Solicitor act against You when you employ them to WIN your case. CORRUPTION...they are NOT the work of God they try to delude. Nothing escapes the truth and I am TRUTH.

Jesus said he was the TRUTH and LIGHT and to trust him...do people really want to improve their life and world or demoralise it?

How do you trust anybody these days Doctor Shipmam was the most notorious serial killer in British history. There is conspiracy linking Michael Jackson's death to Doctors. The Metropolitan Police shot dead a suspected terrorist who was innocent then let sixty terrorists from the I.R.A. back on our streets. Who is kidding who here. If you think this is some joke you are kidding yourself. I know this killing was of course unmeant but why release terrorists, do you really think it safe. I think it is undoing hours of Police work and causing even more corruption.

I hit my ex-partner for sleeping around and was given a custodial sentence and while in H.M.P. Durham we were watching on the News of the Twin Towers (More Conspiracy).

I was arrested for raising my voice in the News and Star office while trying to tell them the story of an escaped terrorist living in my area. It was my Birthday, I had just received a thank you letter from Queen Elizabeth "2nd" and here I was back behind bars. I represent Peace and Prosperity and guess what happens when you take away that...you are left with war and poverty. In this case there was floods in Queensland and murder in my home town.

Conspiracy ...thanks Dad you certainly gave me a story.

Starting rumours and malicious gossip is part of their ploy I think they get off on seeing others hurt. Prim-donnas bring others down to leave themselves looking good and that is what they do.

I would think twice of ever joining such a crew as the Masons, if you tell of their plans you may get killed, what a pity.

The Secret is there is NO Secret.

If you need to know anything it is contained in the Whole or Universal.

Others have been let out of prison and put in my path why they want me dead I may never know, probably jealousy.

Will somebody tell them to desire for others what they desire for themselves or teach them the Delfin Knowledge System, soon please, oh what menaces.

On a more serious side though, if there is one, I love my Dad. He commits no crime, he offered my Mother marriage and I would always buy him a pint. It is more likely that the Council had conspiracy over me. They put me next door to Danny after sacking me as one of their joiners. Or am I being paranoid about the whole events and the truth is more likely the one revealed in Onward Christian Soldiers (S.A.S) Unarmed Combat. How is it that terrorists have been given lighter sentence than murder, for some. I remember the Peace talks allowing some back on to our streets, yet we hung Saddam Hussein. Should we ourselves in Britain give the Death Penalty to our Terrorists. If we did for Sadam Hussein then why not Liam or Danny Heffernan. Liam is to be expected to be released from prison and Danny has just been Captured. Surely what is good for the Goose is good for the Gander. Well let me tell you this Danny ran a blade over my girlfriends privates, how if somebody did that to him. Danny confesses killing, should that happen to him. Of course he escaped while others were caught, he was probably lookout. He has done prison though and only God knows how he is back on our streets. Tougher sentencing is what is required. Maybe we do need a world Government and maybe it should be called the Peace and Prosperity Party. Taking the Laws that work best in each Country. I am thinking that the Laws in Britain's Laws are best when it comes to carrying weapons but I think the Laws in America are best when it comes to murder and terrorism. Danny you need the Death Penalty, he carries weapons and kills, he confesses terrorism and rapes. Why should he have a crust of bread and glass of water. What about all the bullying and poverty. Alcoholics and prostitutes. Where is the good? If it is in Heaven then why not earth? Where is that caring sharing community? Dog eat dog is <u>NOT</u> the answer, the answer is abundantly clear and that is you. You are a production of the Universal, your parents and years of effort. If you hold the truths then you are lucky it has taken me years to find mine. I am almost certain that doctors gave me euthanasia for saying something stupid about killing, I was being abused at the time listening to some heavy confessions, it is hardly surprising I thought of killing I even thought of killing myself. Of course I never carried any of it out but in fact brought my abuser to justice through my previous work. Please forgive me if you think I hold anybody responsible for my life other than me, I do not mean to point the finger but Danny caused commotion in my life. There is good come out of it if only the scripture I have produced. We all need to learn though and I am able to teach the wisest of men just like they can teach me. There was once a hit song called You Learn by Alanis Morriset. You love you learn, you lose you learn and so on we are constantly learning more about ourselves and lives. I never knock anybody without due concern and I am concerned about my children, who I have not seen for years. I say Doctors and Solicitors could have conspiracy but in fact they are more likely to sort it than a terrorist or gangster from the street. I hope it was no set up other than to catch Danny yet I can't help but wonder. I think I have done the deal with God to catch this man. If people were aware of his true ability he would never have been there. In another of Alanis Morriset's songs she sings if only I could kill the killer and believe me that is all I am doing through my work. Yes there are sceptics and each hold our own beliefs. I like the Delfin Knowledge System; my Grandparents liked Freemasons and Farming and my Sons and Daughter like school. Set up or NOT Danny is brought to Justice and looks to be starting his life sentence soon.

It does not stop there though, there is much crime committed where people are CAPTURED, you just need to pick up a Newspaper, it will tell you the same. Criminals are intent on notoriety; I understand the Criminal mind yet have transformed my method of thinking with some of the products from the web-sites below. Crime does NOT pay and every dog gets it day, your time is running out if you are committing today. For the minor offences I have committed is putting a hold on a Criminal Injuries payout to myself and allowing Danny's activity over me, to reign supreme.

REPENT...REPENT...REPENT

I told you I have only met one Angel and she was into heroin and prostitution. I am NOT saying the world is full of serious Criminals but we are born sinners to find forgiveness in Jesus Christ.

REPENT now it is to late on your final day and who knows Heaven may hold a place for YOU.

Imagine the SCENARIO where Shipman was still alive today, would you let him loose with a Terrorist? I certainly would especially Danny Heffernan. A death penalty for terrorism or murder would make people think twice and reduce the amount of serious crime. I once met a man who done six years in prison for attempted murder. Now he tried to kill somebody in a Country where carrying weapons is illegal. What if he did the sentence would have doubled, big deal, he says and tries again. Do you really think he learned from his mistake after six years in prison? Simple black and white DEATH Penalty for Murder or Terrorism then they maybe would think better of it.

World Case Scenario (CAPTURED)

Just think right you are sexually abused, threatened to be killed, have your Grandmother poisoned, witness a dagger ran over your lovers vagina and later find her dead.

You apply for Criminal Injuries but are refused. I hereby enclose a warrant of my criminal activity which most was under diminished responsibility, because of what I witnessed above, see what you think.

My criminal activity, I tell you I am NOT proud of, been reprimanded and have REPENTED. As a child you will be aware you need guidance, well I was let out to play without any, I had free will. I done some stupid things which I will explain. Remember my parents were separated and my Mother tried to bring us up we weren't rich or anything and I had to wait till I reached my hood to commit this crime, according to the God of LOVE.

When I was eight years old I pinched sweets, fuse wire and stupid little things from shops to give to my Mother. She reprimanded me and made me tell the truth were things were coming from, I was only eight with little pocket money and bringing things home which was worth a couple of quid. My Mother new I had no money to buy it but I was telling her I was finding it, she was NOT stupid and sat me on the bottom step of the stairs until she knew the truth. I was scared to tell her so she gave me the best hiding or telling off I had as a child. I told the truth after that and lessons were learned. (Crime punished and REPENTED)

There was a couple of stupid things at ten and eleven fires and trying to drive a motor vehicle. For the fire I was given a caution by Police. For trying to drive a motor vehicle on a public road I was taken to Court paid for the damages and had my licence revoked and endorsed with penalty points.

Both offences (Reprimanded, Punished and Repented)

Then I was caught fishing without a rod licence for my fishing rod taken to court and fined

(Fined and Repented) Stupid LAW anyway.

I was still very young and impressionable and done a couple of other daft things which I have been punished and reprimanded for (Forgive me Lord I know NOT what I do)

Punished and REPENTED

I mean no-matter what I have done does NOT warrant the level of abuse and torture I went through. Now I could understand an axe murderer being refused Criminal Injuries if somebody injured him, but even then if he has done his stretch in prison, could at its extreme pick up a little.

I only ever committed petty crime which I honestly have been reprimanded for and REPENTED but have been on the wrong side of some very serious and Outrageous crime.

Imagine I am your child and I do a few daft things, I am punished and REPENT do I still deserve to be abused sexually at knifepoint, threatened to be killed, have my Grandmother poisoned, see my lover die over a maniac who should never been allowed on the street.

Honestly, you would think NOT.

Well that what the Criminal Injuries department have said and I think it appalling and have asked them to reconsider. You may have already read Onward Christian Soldiers (S.A.S) Unarmed Combat from www.LuLu.com I caught a terrorist and was injured, there you go, is it worth anything? This is what is being debated. What if he was still thinking of the Palace or Lords and Ladies. I have played my part by forwarding information to Police and maybe foiled the plot. Ask yourself this could you do it, would you do it and are you capable of doing it. It took a United Forces to catch Sadam Hussein but it took me to catch The One That Got Away. With God's guidance of course and later the Authorities (Enshala).

Back to LIFE back to REALITY

I am the leader of the Revolutionary...Peace and Prosperity Party. I would give careful consideration of a Death Penalty for attempting such a crime. So would NOT think twice about LIFE imprisonment for Murder or Terrorism and I mean LIFE. The only escape being if you prove your innocence beyond reasonable doubt. Believe me I would rather have the Death Penalty and would ask for the choice to be given. I thought of the offence and thought better of it, but only thought of it because what I witnessed, I remembered my Religious Studies "Though Shall NOT Kill". Even then I REPENT the stupid thought.

I also remember an Eye for an Eye and a Tooth for a Tooth.

I also remember Forgiveness, but where do you draw the line, it must be tough for our Judges making these decisions. Thankfully Doctors, Solicitors and Social Services did me a favour and helped get stability back in my life. I missed out years with my two children but there is hope we will catch that up one day. I plan to assist them in writing a story which will give me greater understanding of their lives, my little babies, tell them from me I love them. Jordan's Home and Lucy's (L.L.Lampshades) will be the titles so I have plenty to look forward to. [(c) 2010 P.N.Dickinson] Jordan's Granddad was an Usher for many years and Lucy's Granddad was a Military Policeman. I have no difference with these but had differences with my ex-partners, so I separated and divorced, but wish the children well.

Karate and Tai-chi

Mind at your mercy and drop kicks to the head. Any body who has met me probably knows a little about me and some of the things they know is Good some is Bad.

Good is overcoming evil, Light is destroying dark, Remember my last work (S.A.S) Unarmed Combat. I attacked the Devil who was a Terrorist, Who was a Murderer, Who was an abuser and who was a Rapist. Light did destroy dark and I messed up his plans. (Thank GOD) (Thank the Carlton Clinic) & (Thank the Police). But my guidance from our Creator Mr. Universal or God and my willingness to be shown a way with www.DelfinGlobal.com or the DELFIN Knowledge System then we are all winners. YES Light really did destroy Dark. I have a close friend who is adept at tai-chi he showed me it one night and boy did it hurt, it is connecting to the Spiritual. I later displayed my Karatte and settled down. Your Spirit protrudes the Physical and some can actually move things without touching it. People like Derryl Brown and Paul McKenna. Paul McKenna, Paul Gascoigne, Paul McCartney and myself are generally good people. Maybe a little daftness from time to time, but Gazza the biggest Paul of all has emotions and will cure one day. Sometimes Paul's knock around with the wrong crowd and seem to take their blame. Good luck Gazza (Paul Gascoigne) you will heal. I once shared the same psychiatric hospital as you, lets cure together we said, were healing are we not.

www.DELFINGlobal.com

Tablets, Meditation and Prayer is a solution to most, Jesus healed the sick, now we have Doctors but we still have the Clergyman.

Relax with a hot drink, meditate by finding stillness of the mind then pray to receive and you shall receive.

We are all of the same mind and origin, brought into the world the same and like Ants scurrying to improve the Kingdom. It is good and generally well preserved. I know I get carried away sometimes but that is my choice, I do not own you but remember you do not own me. God gave man free will and built man in his own image, it is your spirit which is perfect and complete. Yes I was a Soldier Ant and excelled on my mission but dealing with the devil ant (What a mission) do you really think anything is easy and believe me I studied and learned Law by my mistakes of ignorance and while under a diminished state of mind. Not knowing whether to turn left or right at the end of the Garden Path. Danny should pay my injuries it is him to blame not the Government, at least JUSTICE will be done, Ce La Vi...Life goes on. I will never withdraw my claim though. I suppose Ireland just want their own Country but what gives Danny the right to sexually abuse and kill? He is NOT beyond the LAW. His stupidity may cost his life or at least a life sentence. Silly little man. The Female of the species is more deadly than the male and the way he is with woman he needs psychiatric care with one of the female doctors. He ran a blade over my girlfriends vagina for GOD SAKE.

I would challenge him to a boxing match, he is far from hard, just dangerous with weapons.

For all the confusion and disruption to my life and world I could take the Kings Ransom, but I leave that for the state to decide, I would like is £1,000,000 (Millionaire STATUS) and a George Cross. Although I will settle for the biggest Criminal Injuries payout ever and the George Cross with Danny given a Life to Life sentence. He is a ringleader and will prevent further dangers to society if he is taken away.

Now with the REST of World Case Scenario (CAPTURED) create your own Perfect Picture with the Cut out and keep characters & figures from the remaining of this work.

Create the PERFECT PICTURE

The winner of the Perfect Picture competition wins a top prize by posting them to e-mail: pndevelopments@hotmail.co.uk

GOOD LUCK

While this work and the CLEARER PICTURE may sound like their has been conspiracy over my life it is totally unprovable.

The truths surrounding this story is more likely that Paul went in search of a Newspaper clipping as revealed within

(S.A.S) Unarmed Combat www.LuLu.com

Check my other work at www.YouTube.com

(Search) Octowarriors R Us includes

Peace and Prosperity Party Speech

Assistance and guidance through the studies of the DELFIN Knowledge System and was produced to try to assist in a safer community.

Create YOUR Perfect Picture with the cut out and keep collage figures from the following pages. For the biggest and best PERFECT PICTURE will Win a prize.

Think of its title, play and have fun. (Good Luck)

Angel Paris Jordan

GarTrader

"Hello... I'm calling to check your pacemaker."

"Hello... I'm calling to check your pacemaker."

For your B.I.G.A. picture...For Your Clearer picture...For Your Perfect Picture log onto www.LuLu.com

Octowarriors to add to your Perfect Picture available from the B.I.G.A. picture collection plus other images available from the CLEARER PICTURE.

Good Luck with your Journey & have fun.

The TRUTH is out there TAKE CARE.

If you feel as though you are mentioned within this work, we thank you for your trust and wish you well in life, including Masons, Doctors and Solicitors. GOOD over EVIL Only exclusion Deluded Dan who is (CAPTURED) right throughout all my written work. World Case Scenario (CAPTURED).

The B.I.G.A. picture as (The Highland Beaver)

The CLEARER PICTURE as (Deluded Dan)

Onward Christian Soldiers

(S.A.S) Unarmed Combat as (The Welder) & (Jock the Scott)

The B.I.G.A. (CLEARER) Perfect Picture is really your choice.

The winner of this competition will take half of the collective funds drawn soon.

The theme is bringing Danny Boy (The Dodgy car dealer to justice)

Some of your images are contained in the B.I.G.A. picture, some in the CLEARER PICTURE and the remaining right here in your Perfect Picture. www.LuLu.com

Also see S.A.S. Unarmed Combat at www.LuLu.com

Entry fee £100 or proof of purchase of the World Case Scenario (Captured)

For competition Purposes we WILL allow images ONLY to be transmitted or photocopied with the preservation of the book in mind.

This book was produced in Honour to my Mother & Father, Sister & Brother, Son & Daughter, God & Jesus, Doctors & Nurses, Policemen & Woman, Masons & NOT and for You.

My Name is Paulie Dee and I have a FEW Good ideas for Anneka U Cee...

(1) Anneka's Airwaves

(Fruity Filled Gum leaving a Minty Fresh Taste)

(2) The Annie/KA with Ford Car and Annie Stickers including Doctor with Bag.

(3) SUPA Specs (Optician) Because we all see through a Different Lens.

Angel and Paulie Dee

Peace and Prosperity

(Search) One Mind Trilogy...B.I.G.A. picture www.lulu.com

(Search) PaulNigel10 with 10 out of 10 www.YouTube.com

For Danny it was the Death Penalty....(Starter for TEN)

One Down TEN to Go.

Training to be a Doctor was the Next Step for our Young S.A.S representative and he became Doctor Dickie or Doctor Dolphin in Surgery Times.

The Day I took One and TEN... S.A.S.

Doctor Dolphin had Given Danny his Lethal Injection and then realized there was much more out there than One Terrorist.

A debate over TEN more was Granted.

One Way TICKET To HELL

(1) *Thomas O'Neil*

(2) *Norman (KAZZA) McKaskie*

(3) *Onur Quataba*

(4) *Brian Miller*

(5) *John (Crocket) Peel*

(6) *Nigel Miller*

(7) *Alan Muse*

(8) *Stuart Smith*

(9) *Adrian Miller*

(10) *Terrence Edward O'Neil*

The Butter MELTED in Anneka's Mouth...

They are all Paranoid Schizophrenics Anneka said to Doctor Dickie, YES who have links to I.R.A and Al-Kieda.

Doctor Dickie pulled on Doctor Dolphin and the Injection was administered of Clinical Euthanasia.

There is always One that Gets away.

Liam Heffernan can be seen behind Bars on the Cover of World Case Scenario (Captured) @ www.LuLu.com.

The B.I.G.A., The Clearer, The Perfect Picture

(c) Copyright 2010

Written by P. N. Dickinson

www.LuLu.com

All rights reserved. No part of this book may be reproduced or transmitted in any form nor by any means, electronic, mechanical, photographic or phonographic process, nor may be stored in a retrieval system, or otherwise be copied for public or private use other than for "fair use" as brief quotations embodied in articles and reviews, without prior written permission of the copyright holder and publisher. We hold no responsibility for your actions and my work is forbidden from any terrorist or murderer. Images may be used or copied for competition purposes in order to restore your book but you should have proof of entry for every Perfect Picture which is entered.

This work was produced for FUN although deals with a serious issue and should only be looked as though a young Christian S.A.S Soldier (CAPTURES) an escaped Terrorist.

Have fun creating your Perfect Picture or Collage then e-mail Your work to pndevelopments@hotmail.co.uk for entry into our new competition.

OutLawing the Seven Deadly Sins.

Tax

Baby Dangling

Freemasonry

Laws of Adoption

Doctrine

Judge Deluding

Voyeurism

Replaced with Free the Weed (With Guidelines) (21+ Avoid Alcohol)

Waiting in the

WINGS

The Day we took

One and TEN

S.A.S

He & She who

DARES WON

(WONDER Boy)

I would TAKE on a
HUNDRED More
I know the Score
S.A.S
123 Declared NOT Out
ButHIT for SIX.
Thats CRICKET.
MAYHEM...

124 We know the Score.

(c) Copyright: P.N.Dickinson 2012

Paul was Carted off to the Carleton where he was Diagnosed with Sleep Deprivation and Suicidal Depression due to his Dealings with Twelve of the most Notorious Criminals to have lived.

Injuries and Loss are being Reviewed.

(Search) Bob Dylan ... Knocking on Heavens' Door www.YouTube.com

Carted to the Carleton then transferred to St. Nicholas hospital we witnessed more MAYHEM.

Hospitals full of ill People and some even Dangerous....Mayhem.

The Author of this book (Part 5) Pent-O-Gramme would like to take this Opportunity to thank all those who helped and Guided him through this sincere MAYHEM.

My Children, who I hope have it a little easier than I, I will LOVE Eternally (Jordan & Lucy)

I hope my Parents find true Happiness knowing their Son has Lived through this Mayhem and become STRONGER AND STRONGER.

I wish the Police and Doctors all they look for out of LIFE and thank them for taking on this Difficult CASE.

I thank the LORD who Shone his Light when Mayhem was winning.

I wish the Monarchs and Queen every Success knowing of their innocence.

Thank the Government for providing a Basic Income which allowed me the time to complete this work.

I also thank you for your Custom and understanding through all this MAYHEM.

THANK YOU

MAYHEM

(Part Five) Pent-O-Gramme

My Name is Paulie dee i have the final three Good Ideas to see...

(1) *Custard corners with Fruit and Crumble*
(2) *Fruitie Loopies (Sweets)*
(3) *The Face Fits (T.V) Show Ten Faces, One Voice, Three contestants.*

Copyright of Pent-O-Gramme and One Mind Trilogy ideas may be used at 50% Pro-fit Margin to...
PaulieDee80@yahoo.com
Thanks

+1 Childrens Slot Mint Machine (Accepts and pays in Polo's or Trebor Mints

MI-NT-ED (Jackpot)
MAYHEM
The END

www.ingramcontent.com/pod-product-compliance
Lightning Source LLC
Chambersburg PA
CBHW030814310726
48980CB00006B/489/J

* 9 7 8 1 4 7 1 7 9 3 2 9 5 *